To The Girls I Once Was

Apoorva Krishna Rao

ISBN: 9798531388896

To all the people I trusted to read and listen to my terrible first drafts.

And to anyone who has never known where they belonged.

A special shoutout to my cousin, Megha, the first poet in the family who, without my even knowing, helped me believe anyone could write. This is for dedicating a book to me.

CONTENTS

ACKNOWLEDGMENTS

This is to everyone who supported me, whether they knew it or not. Some of my friends didn't even know I was making this but they kept me going. I've received so much support even from people who are basically strangers. I am so grateful to everyone in my life, whether they knew about this book or not.

This is to you, if you have ever shown me kindness, if you are reading these words.

TW: Mentions of suicidal ideation and self harm

Winter - Grief

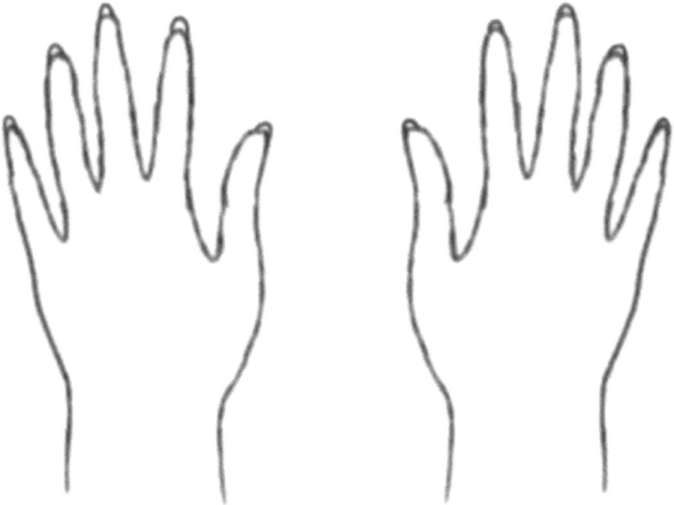

To That Winter Girl

This is
To that winter night.
To the snowflakes that fell.
And to the cheeks that pinked.

The clouds grew heavy,
Rain turned to snow,
That blew over cities,
And the flakes flew faster.

They flew and flew and flew
And what are we if not snowflakes?
And what are we if not ice and frost?
And what are we if not thawing silver?

So to that winter girl, I ask
Do you still feel too heavy to go on?
Do you still feel nothing but gray?
Do you still feel as if you are covered in ice that you could not possibly thaw?

Because, although the Clouds would keep moving,
And the Snow would slowly melt,
And the Rain would keep falling,
And the Seasons would change,

The Clouds would no longer be so unabashedly beautiful,
The Snow would not thaw so graciously,
The Rain would not pour so ferociously,
And the Seasons would not move on so quickly.

So to that winter girl, I ask
Do you finally feel light?
Do you finally feel the world in color?
Do you finally feel the ice thawing?

Locked

I've never been able to sit alone with myself
in pure silence,
too many things to think of,
too much pain.

It makes it hard to sleep sometimes,
that never ending murmur.
Because it can turn to more,
until I am entirely stuck.

In a prison
of my own making, of course.
I just wish
I could find the key.

Alone

Glances at night,
Whispers in the dark,
Movements in the shadows,
Things scurry where there is no light,
Footsteps thud across forgotten rooms.

In my mind?
Or something more?
Is it here to remind me
of something I can't ignore?
In my mind, I am confined.

Night falls,
Darkness shifts,
Shadows speak,
Light abandons,
All alone once more.

Like a Bird

A bird flew by.

Someone walks in,
a plastered smile,
her mind begins to spin.

They leave
and she lets her smile drop.
No longer able to believe
her mind would stop.

Leaving behind the empty halls,
she looks below, at the open sea.
Her stomach falls
and then, so does she.

Vision blurred,
finally free,
like a bird.

Except she could never fly.

Remember

"It's a bad day, not a bad life"
And I wish I could remember that.
I wish I could remember,
when I need it most.

A moment is not a day
is not a week
is not a year
is not a life.

But that's really
really hard
to remember,
when the world feels like it's about to end.

And that's
the farthest thing
from my mind
when I want to end it.

I know I never would
never could.
But that doesn't stop the thoughts.
The thoughts

that turn it from
a bad moment
to a bad day
to a bad week.

I just
wish I could remember.
I just
need to remember.

Broken Promises

You keep saying you'll do it.
"Later"
"Tonight"
"Tomorrow".

But it's always "later",
I just want you to put me first for once
help me now
not in twenty, not tomorrow, now.

And I don't want to be needy,
but I keep waiting,
and this happens
every. single. time.

I try to say something
why do I believe you anymore?
I just set myself up
and you say I'm being dramatic.

You never really understood
It was never about broken promises
It was always about
broken hearts.

Feel

I don't remember the specifics of a situation
but I do remember how it made me feel.

I remember being locked in a dark room,
I don't remember why
but I know I was terrified.

I remember being told I was sick,
I don't remember how
but I know I was confused.

I remember you telling me I wasn't enough,
and I don't remember the words
but I know I hated myself.

I remember how you have made me feel
but I still don't know why.

Labels

We were never really anything.
We never had a label.
We weren't best friends
or dating.

But it sure as hell felt like something.
Like our lives were entwined.
So I'm not sure
how we just stopped.

Stopped talking.
Stopped saying "hey" when we ran into one another.
Stopped knowing each other.
Stopped loving.

Because we were a part
of each other's lives.
And I don't know
how that just ends.

Transitions

I thought it would
feel different,
full of hope,
that transition.

A weight lifted off my shoulders.
Finally free of commitments I never wanted,
a million things I can now do
but it still feels like I'm trapped.

Now,
all I feel
is a strange sense
of emptiness.

Empty

I often feel like I'm waiting.
Waiting for the world,
waiting for something to change,
waiting to disappear.

But, like forgotten copper,
there's a feeling of dullness.
Like I am made of nothing.

When it feels like there is absolutely nothing
to do—nothing I want to do,

I often feel like I am disappearing.

Something

The world feels empty,
I'm not sure how to fix it,
I'm not sure I want to try.

It's not that I don't want to be happy,
it's that I'm not sure how.

Because how am I supposed to go about that?
How am I supposed to figure out
how to be happy?

It sure feels
a hell of a lot
easier
to just give up.

To let the world
pass you by,
sit aside,
and let it happen.
Let the world continue.

Without you.

To let the world
keep spinning,
and spinning,
and simply let it pass.
Let it leave you behind.

Because at least then,
it wouldn't just be emptiness.
It would be
something.

And I'm just looking for something.

Dream

I used to dream
of what I wanted to be.
The things I would do
when I was finally free.

And yet,
it's been 8 years.
And still,
I'm awash in fears

Because maybe I still can't do
all that I used to dream.
The job I wanted,
the things I used to scheme.

How I dreamt
of owning a bookstore,
changing the world.
But I'm not even at the ground floor.

I'm screaming at the top of my lungs,
but nobody seems to hear.
It's still not enough.
Essentially, intentionally, absolutely—bottom tier.

And 17 is still young.
But what can I do,
when the world seems to think
I have no clue

about the things
I dream to do?

She

She was everything I could never be.
The sun and the moon,
blazing orange,
and pearly white.

She radiated beauty,
inspired passion,
demanded to be loved,
and she deserved to be.

Because she made you feel beautiful too.
And she made you feel more passion than you'd ever seen.
And it was everything to be loved by her.
And it was everything, to feel like you deserved her.

But I wonder,
what must that do to someone?
To know that you were the person that was written into legends,
what must that do to you?

Melting silver,
burning ice,
moon and sun alike.
But maybe, she was everything I never wanted to be either.

These Four Walls

These four walls,
covered in posters, pictures, plants, and paintings,
have seen more of me
than anyone else.

But they keep my secrets,
when I've cried myself to sleep,
screamed until my voice gave out,
and worst of all,

as I sat in silence.
In those moments
where even getting out of bed
felt like too much.

And these four
olive green walls
have stayed with me,
even in that silence.

They have helped.
I'm not sure how,
but I do know
they have helped to hold me up.

The Lone Mourner

I met a traveler from an antique land.
He said, "Turn back! All that awaits is despair and misery!"
"Do not fear sire!" I told him, traversing through the sand,
"If I continue, my name will go down in history."

I continue walking, the sand sucking in my feet.
A town arises over the horizon,
And there my eyes meet:
A city razed, under the sand rising,

A single house, all that remains
A brown disheveled hut
A lone cry across the plains
A door slams shut

Empty eyes, bare feet
A little girl crouched in the corner,
Covered by a thin sheet,
Was the lone mourner.

She was me.

Summer - Yearning

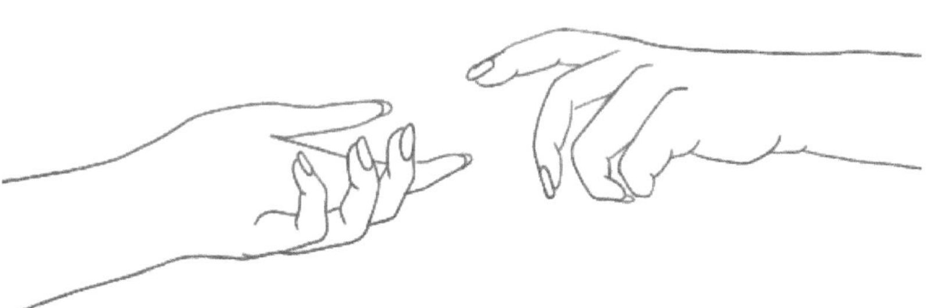

To That Summer Girl

This is
To that summer night.
To the stars that winked.
And to the moths that flew to the light.

The stars are ever-evolving.
They burn,
Collapse,
And are reborn.

They are born and born and born.
And what are we if not the remnants of stars reborn?
And what are we if not the rebirth of galaxies?
And what are we if not the culmination of the universe?

So to that summer girl, I ask
Are you still unhappy?
Are you still aching?
Are you still yearning?

Because, although the Stars will keep moving,
And the Earth will keep spinning,
And the Night will keep falling,
And the Day will keep coming,

The Stars would not wink so brightly,
The Earth would not breathe so lightly,
The Night would not be so calm,
And the Day would not be so bright.

So to that summer girl, I ask
Are you finally happy?
Are you finally content?
Are you finally who you want to be?

Still Learning

I miss seeing the world
through rose-colored glasses.

I miss not seeing the world
and how bad it could be.

I grew up too fast
I miss the way I once lived.

I grew up too fast
but so did a lot of us.

I missed the chance to just be a kid
and I am still learning how to be okay.

I Still Miss You

I still remember
your laugh,
how I swapped our lunches because I wanted you to eat,
how I loved you.

I still remember
how you texted me every day,
your favorite songs,
how you made me laugh.

And I still miss you
like the moon misses the sun in the morning skies,
and I still think about,
the good moments.

But I am still learning
to let you go,
to accept the loss, the good, the bad,
and move on.

Moss to Stone Walls

I cling to people
like moss to stone walls.
Impossible to remove, yes,
but also

without reason
or a care if it's what I need.
Because sometimes it's easier
to hold on.

Easier than to let go
and find somewhere else.
But sometimes
it's better to do what's hard,

to let go from where you're not wanted,
and go somewhere you are
where you're tended to,
cared for.

But the problem is that knowing
doesn't make it any easier.
Because moss clings to stone walls
without reason.

Fame

I feel like everyone has wanted
to be famous at some point.
I know I have,
but I'm not sure why.

Maybe it's the idea
that something about me
could be worthwhile,
some reason I would be famous.

Is it the idea of being adored, of being loved?
Is it the idea of having money to spend and give?
Or is it the idea of finally having a purpose?
I feel like I just want a different life.

And maybe it would be nice
to have people you don't even know
admiring you from afar
when your own world seems so devoid of it.

Cut Fruit

I have heard people say
"Asian moms cut fruit
that's how they apologize,
how they say I love you."

Yes, now I get it
and I am grateful
for the ways she
has learned to speak to me.

But it's not the same.
Not when you're young,
not when you need more,
not when you don't even love yourself.

yes,
love may be stored
in the cut fruit
she brings me,
but,
growing up
it would have meant
everything…
if only
i could just hear those words, too.

"i'm sorry"
"i was wrong"
"i love you"
"i am proud of you."

and love may be stored
in the cut fruit.
but it took me years
to find it.

“Sorry”

It’s a never ending cycle,
the same old script,
just recycled
and it’s exhausting to decrypt.

Because I know
what happens the next day.
“I’m sorry” although,
it never seems to stay that way.

And I am sick and tired,
of believing you would change.
Sometimes “sorry”
isn’t enough.

I just want you to realize
“sorry” doesn’t mean “I want your forgiveness”,
“sorry” means “I’ll try harder, I’ll be better”
and all I have ever wanted is for you to try.

Used To

I miss when I didn't miss anything,
when I didn't yearn to see that friend
I haven't spoken to in years.

I miss when I used to talk to my middle school best friend,
when we would write "I love you" every day
I haven't seen her in years.

I miss that boy I used to talk to every day,
when we would swear we were going to game "tomorrow"
I don't remember the last time we talked.

I miss the days they didn't invade my dreams,
when I wouldn't wake up, thinking I should text them
I don't think I'll ever reach out, though.

And I miss the months I didn't think they hated me,
when I would just enjoy their company
because I wasn't wondering why they would just leave me.

I miss the lives I used to lead.

To Live

There is so much to life
that I have yet to experience,
I used to think I never could,
but I was wrong. I can.

I want to go to cafes with my friends,
even though I hate coffee.

I want to have a "spot",
that is just ours.

I want to sneak out,
in the middle of the night.

I want to write bad music and even worse poems,
just because I can.

I want to live,
without worrying about what someone else will think.

I will have those experiences,
one day,
I want to live
because I was never allowed to.

Almost Home

I haven't been back to India
in nearly 10 years.
I still miss
all the beautiful little eccentricities.

How lizards would crawl up the walls
as you tried to fall asleep.
How there would always be a constant murmur
from people coming and going.

A different continent,
a different culture,
a different world,
and still, I felt at peace.

There is something beautiful
about going back to a home
that isn't really home,
something celestial.

It's like going back to visit a school
you once went to.
A homesickness of what could have been,
the things I missed,

the things I forgot,
but there is something comforting
about going back
to an almost home.

Island in the Storm

It's still thundering,
my world shakes with every rumble.
I don't know when it will stop,
if it will at all.

But I'm still stranded during this storm.
And my heart beats, loud as thunder,
my breath as fast as the wind
pelting my already-stained cheeks.

And I'm still searching
for my island in the storm,
a safe haven,
but I don't know how to find it.

I'm looking,
I'm not even sure
if it exists,
but I'll keep searching.

I'm unsure of what it is I'm looking for.
But I am sure there is something.
And I won't give up
on my island in the storm.

Mine

If you were mine,

I would text you good morning
and good night, every day.

I would buy you flowers
and put them behind your ear.

I would bring you coffee
and remember just how you like it.

I would help you with homework
and stay up late studying with you.

I would celebrate your wins
and console you after your losses.

But you aren't mine,

and I haven't even found you yet.

Souls

I don't want to start
with small talk.
I want to get down to your soul,
to the parts of you you don't love enough.

So, tell me your favorites.
Send me your 3 a.m. poems.
Show me how you see the world,
and see me too.

Tell me your hates too.
Send me your late night notes, filled with pain.
Show me how you love,
and love me too.

I want to start
with the deep down truths of us.
And I don't want to be a mystery either,
so I will give you my soul, too.

Traces

I have left traces of who I am,
everywhere I've been.
Like carving my initials into soft marble,
as if I am claiming "look at me, this is who I am".

And I let people do the same to me,
for I have traces of all the people I have ever loved.
They have made their mark, like graffiti on highway walls
like I want to say "look at me, this is who I have loved".

Their marks stay,
long after they have gone.
But that's okay
because some part of them stays with me too.

And I don't want to forget,
even if it hurts.
I don't want to paint over
the traces of their fading graffiti.

Wind

Sometimes it feels like I'm traversing
through a barren tundra.
I keep looking back,
hoping to see someone

calling out to me
"please, don't go"
"talk to us"
"are you okay? at least tell us where you're going."

But they never come.
The only sound is the gusting wind
as it continues to try to blow me down.
It drowns out everything else.

I keep waiting,
praying they'll call for me.
But they never come,
or at least I don't think they did.

And no matter
how much I hope,
how much I wish,
I'm not sure I would ever hear it.

Because the wind drowns out anything else.

Fire and Ice - Acceptance

To the Girl of Fire and Ice

This is to the girl
Who didn't quite know who she was,
Who she had been,
Or who she wanted to be.

The days passed,
Tests were aced, and failed,
Friends were hung out with,
Conversations were had.

But it all felt like floating through limbo.
Like it was just doing the motions
Trying to find some semblance of life
Trying to live, not just survive.

So to that girl of fire and ice, I ask
What was I supposed to have done?
What was I supposed to do when the world didn't feel full of possibility?
What was I supposed to do when even the motions felt like too much?

Because, although the World would continue on,
And the Sun would keep rising,
And Music would keep playing,
And Poetry would still be read,

The World would not be the same,
The Sun would not be as warm,
And there are so many Songs you have not yet heard,
And hundreds of Poems you have yet to write.

So to that girl of fire and ice, I ask
Do you know what you need to do?
Does the world feel like it's no longer covered in ice?
Do the motions finally feel like they are full of fire?

Promises (Fire and Ice)

I used to
make promises to myself,
of things I would do,
places I would go,
people I would be.

They were never very real,
just there to tide me over
until I could heal
make a new deal
and start once more.

But I send a promise into the air
I would one day, take the bad with the good,
I would keep the promises I made when it was too much
to bear.
I still remember, the clothes I wanted to wear,
the books I wanted to read,

the world I wanted to change,
and the me I no longer wanted to be.
But it still felt strange,
and my emotions would range
from confusion to emptiness.

But I learned to take
the bad with the good.
Both the happiness and the never-ending ache,
and even now, sometimes I still wake
not knowing if I can take on the day.

The world is hard
and it often doesn't make sense
I sometimes still hold my breath, waiting to find a shard
of the person I once was, still scarred.
But I have promised to always take the bad with the good.

Missed Train

Sometimes it feels
like I've missed the train to where I'm supposed to be.
Sometimes it feels
like I've missed the way to the rest of my life.

One decision
I shouldn't have made.
One decision
I couldn't have known.

Would change everything
that I thought I knew.
Would change everything
I still don't know, if it was for better or worse.

But I think
I might never know.
But I think
I don't need to know.

One decision can't change
everything, because I am still me.
One decision can't change
that I will always be me.

The person I've become
no matter what I've gone through.
The person I've become
will always be under the surface, making themself known.

Rejected

rejected. rejected. rejected.
by people,
by organizations,
by myself.

It hurts.
I won't tell you it doesn't,
because it does.
But the pain fades.

It becomes
that person you once liked,
that opportunity you heard of,
that bad summer.

Because every rejection has changed me,
taught me about relationships,
opened a new door,
helped me accept myself.

Without them, I would not
love the same people,
have the same wants,
or know who I am.

Boundaries

You joke about my trauma,
like it's yours.
Like you have a right to it.

As if you have ever
gone through it,
or lived my life.

It is not yours
just because
you know me.

It is not yours
just because
you have watched me go through it.

It is not yours
just because
I don't know how to stand up for myself.

But I am growing,
and one day
I will change that,

I will stand up
and I will say something
because my trauma is not yours,
no matter how much of it you have seen.

Healing

I am healing.

I forgot the number
for the suicide prevention hotline.

I stopped flinching
at every pair of scissors I saw shine.

I learned to stop worrying
every time someone would scoff.

I started sleeping
with the lights off.

I allowed myself
to stop being so tough.

I finally realized
that maybe I could be enough.

But healing is a never ending process.

Bystander

"Just calm down" they say
after they initiated.

"Relax, you need to take a breath"
a smirk playing on their lips.

So I "take a breath", gather my things,
and leave.

I let myself "calm down"
try to "relax"

and then I go back
"always running away" they scoff.

And I realize, it's not that I'm too much.
It is that I have stopped sitting silently by.
No longer a bystander in my own life.

Strangers

A shuffle of feet,
a hurried apology,
a glance across the tracks,
a smile as we cross each other's lives.

I wonder how many strangers' lives I've been a part of?
How many people have wanted something of mine,
an outfit, a hairstyle, an experience?
Because I know I have admired people from afar.

I wonder what my passing beauty is,
all strangers have it.
The way they walk,
how they bob their head to music,

Something inherently lovable.
And it took me a while to realize
that meant that I had something too.
Something that made me inherently lovable.

Sitting in Silence

There's something
beautifully intimate
about sitting in silence
with someone you love.

Like I'm baring my soul,
without saying a word.
We can somehow see each other's flaws,
but we don't say a thing.

And it is in those
beautifully intimate moments,
sitting, acknowledging, accepting,
I can also come to love myself.

Who

It took me a long while
to start figuring out
who I am.
But I'm done shying away from it.

So I swear,
I am going to learn
who I am
and embrace it.

I love wisteria
and hate coffee.

Reading is my escape
from my current prison.

Poetry is my catharsis
but I can be the cause of my own greatest pain.

I could go on,
but I'm still learning
who I am
and who I want to be.

Life

I don't want to wake up
and have had life pass me by.

I don't want to wake up
and one day realize I never lived how I wanted.

I don't want to wake up
and regret how I lived.

I am slowly realizing
life isn't about money or looking a certain way.

Life is about experiences
and learning.

Life is about love
and loving and being loved.

Life is about more than anyone will ever be able to say
and that is beautiful in and of itself.

So I changed the way I lived
I started living for me.

So this is a promise,
I will dance in the rain,
I will run through open fields,
~~I will stay up reading until I can barely see,~~
I will scream sing with my friends as we drive at midnight,
~~I will jump on my bed at 2 a.m.,~~
I will scream into oblivion,
I will stop caring about what everyone else thinks.

Again and again and again,
I will choose me.

Self-Perception (Fire and Ice)

I have loved
and been loved.
But there is something entirely different
about loving yourself.

I was talking to my therapist
and he asked me to speak to myself
as if I was talking to a friend
whenever I felt negatively about myself.

I realized,
in that moment
how we see ourselves through a skewed lens
how horribly we abuse ourselves.

"fat"
"thin lips"
"big thighs"
"stretch marks"
"big nose"
I could go on.

But there is nothing inherently ugly
about any of those qualities.
We even admire them in our friends.
So why is it when we look at ourselves, we are so utterly
disappointed in what we find?

And yes I am still trying,
But sometimes I can't. Sometimes it's too hard
to love all the aspects I see as flaws.
But trying is better than nothing.

Hidden

She used to
cover her mouth when she laughed,
use her hair as a shield,
wear clothes she hated.

Desperate
to stay hidden,
out of the spotlight,
because she was never

good enough,
bright enough,
pretty enough.
Enough.

And now,
she laughs loudly,
filled with love.
She ties her hair up.

Because her confidence is her shield,
her clothes are her expression,
and she no longer
needs to stay hidden.

I am Proud of You

I am proud of you
for the love you have chosen
over and over again.
Even when it gets to be too much.

I am proud of you
for choosing life
every day.
Even when it feels like the world is screaming at you.

I am proud of you
for choosing to continue
every minute.
Even when it seems like the hardest decision.

And I am so proud of you,
for continuing to be yourself
every second.
Even when it isn't easy.

Acceptance.

The moon fades
and the sun rises,
rain leaves behind
early morning dew.

And I don't pause to think
as I step outside,
breathing in
the fresh morning wind.

Finally forgetting my hesitations,
allowing myself to just be
as the wet lawns
graze my feet

and the rains begin again.
But for once,
I allow myself to throw my head back and dance,
instead of rushing back inside.

www.ingramcontent.com/pod-product-compliance
Ingram Content Group UK Ltd.
Pitfield, Milton Keynes, MK11 3LW, UK
UKHW042001190726
13854UKWH00005B/2095

9 798531 388896